# Katie Woo

NO LONGER PROPERTY OF
Seattle Public Library

Every Day's
an Adventure

by Fran Manushkin
illustrated by Tammie Lyon

capstone

Katie Woo is published by Picture Window Books
A Capstone Imprint
1710 Roe Crest Drive
North Mankato, MN 56003
www.capstonepub.com

Library of Congress Cataloging-in-Publication Data
Manushkin, Fran.
  Katie Woo, every day's an adventure / by Fran Manushkin; illustrated by Tammie Lyon.
     pages cm. — (Katie Woo)
  Summary: In these four previously published stories, Katie Woo has her first ride in an airplane, her first horse ride, and enjoys other new adventures.
  ISBN 978-1-4795-5211-5 (pbk.)
1. Woo, Katie (Fictitious character)—Juvenile fiction. 2. Chinese American families—Juvenile fiction. 3. Chinese Americans—Juvenile fiction. [1. Family life—Fiction. 2. Chinese Americans—Fiction.] I. Lyon, Tammie, illustrator. II. Title. III. Title: Katie Woo, every day is an adventure. IV. Title: Every day's an adventure. V. Series: Manushkin, Fran. Katie Woo.
  PZ7.M3195Kbgk 2014
  813.54—dc23                                    2014004765

Photo Credits
Greg Holch, pg. 96; Tammie Lyon, pg. 96

Designer: Kristi Carlson

Printed in Canada.
032014   008086FRF14

# Table of Contents

# Cowgirl Katie

Katie was reading about cowgirls.

They looked so happy on their horses.

"Yippie-yi-yo!" Katie sang. "Riding a horse looks cool!"

"Guess what I want for my birthday?" said Katie. "A horse! I'll feed him carrots and ride him in the yard."

"Our yard is too small," said
Katie's mom. "Horses need a field, and
they cost a lot of money."

"I have money in my piggy bank,"
said Katie.

But it was not enough.

Katie told JoJo, "If I had a horse,
I'd ride as fast as the wind!"

"Horses are big," said JoJo. "I
might be afraid to ride one."

"Not me," said Katie.

Katie wrote a poem in her journal:

"I want a horse!

I do! Of course.

I'd ride it all day,

Up, up, and away!"

Katie pretended her bike was a
horse.

"Giddy-up!" she shouted.

But her bike didn't have a mane
and a tail.

Katie rode a horse on the merry-go-round.

"Giddy-up!" she yelled.

The horse had a mane and a tail, but they were made of wood.

Katie collected horse stickers and put them everywhere.

Pedro teased her, "You are horse crazy."

"You bet!" said Katie.

One day, Katie's dad said, "I have a
surprise. I am taking you to a ranch."

"Will I ride a horse?" asked Katie.

"Yes!" said her dad. "JoJo and
Pedro are coming too."

They got into their van and rode
to the ranch.

"Hello, horses!" Katie yelled.
"Wow! You sure are big!"

Pedro and JoJo got on their horses. But Katie said, "Wait! First I want to give my horse a carrot."

The horse liked the carrot. He nuzzled Katie with his big head.

"Come on!" yelled JoJo. "Get on
your horse and ride with us!"

"I better not," said Katie. "My horse looks tired. He wants to rest."

"Katie," said her mom, "when I was little, I was scared of horses."

"You were?" said Katie. "I'm a little worried. My horse is so high up."

"He is," said Katie's dad. "But I'll
be holding on to you."

"You will?" said Katie. "That would
be great!"

Katie got on the horse.

"Whoo!" Katie said. "Here I go!"

Her horse began walking slowly.

"Let's go faster," said Katie. So the horse began trotting!

"Ride 'em, cowgirl!" Pedro yelled.

"I'm riding!" shouted Katie. "I'm riding!"

Katie sang a cowgirl song:

"I like this horse.

I do! Of course!

I could ride all day!

Yippee-yi-yo! Hurray!"

After the ride, Katie gave her horse
a hug and said, "Thank you! I'll never
forget you."

"Katie," said her mom, "you were very brave."

"I know," said Katie. "I'm a cowgirl. We are always brave — most of the time!"

# Fly High, Katie!

Pedro was showing Katie his model airplane.

"I'm going to Florida," said Katie. "Soon I'll be flying, too."

"No way," teased Pedro. "Your arms will get tired."

"You are silly!" said Katie. "I'm flying in an airplane. It's my first time."

"Flying is fun," said JoJo. "You'll love it."

Katie and her mom and dad hurried to the airport. They each had a suitcase. Katie also had her teddy bear.

They rushed to the counter to
check their suitcases, then waited in a
long line to get on the plane.

"When will this be fun?" Katie
wondered.

Finally, they got on the plane. As Katie buckled her seat belt, she said, "I wonder if my teddy bear needs a seat belt too?"

Katie reached for her bear, but he wasn't there!

"Where's Teddy?" she asked.

"I don't know," said her mom. "He was with us when we checked in."

"We have to run back and get him!" cried Katie.

"We can't," said her dad. "The plane is about to take off."

*Zoom!* The plane sped down the runway. Then it flew up, up, UP!

Everything on the ground got smaller and smaller.

"Poor Teddy," said Katie. "You are all alone down there."

Katie watched the clouds floating by. One looked like a tiger, and one looked just like Teddy.

Katie's mom gave her some orange
juice. Whoops! The plane hit a bump,
and the juice spilled on her lap.

"Yikes!" yelled Katie. "What a
mess!"

"JoJo told me that flying is fun," groaned Katie. "Maybe it is for birds, but not for me. And I miss my Teddy so much."

"Folks," said the captain, "buckle your seat belts. We will be flying through some turbulence."

"What's that?" asked Katie.

"That's when air gets bumpy," said Katie's mom.

The plane began rocking up and down.

"Wow!" Katie smiled. "This is like riding a pony. It's fun!"

"Soon you'll be seeing Grandma," said Katie's dad. "That will be fun too."

"For sure!" agreed Katie.

After a while, the ride was smooth again. Katie saw trees and a pretty river shining in the sun. She drew a picture to show Pedro and JoJo.

"We are almost there," said Katie's mom.

The plane flew lower and lower — and *whoosh* — they were back on the ground!

"Where is my suitcase?" Katie
wondered.

"You'll see," said her dad. "Follow
me."

"The suitcases will be coming out here," said Katie's dad. "It's called a carousel because it goes round and round."

Katie watched for her bag. She waited . . . and waited.

And what did she see? Teddy!

He looked happy to see her too.

"So that's where he went," said

Katie's dad. "He was checked in with

our suitcases."

"And here's Grandma," shouted Katie.

She hugged Teddy and Grandma tight.

"This vacation will be great," said Katie.

It already was.

# Katie and the Fancy Substitute

Katie hurried to school.

She loved school, and she loved
her teacher, Miss Winkle.

But Miss Winkle wasn't there.
"Good morning," said a new
person. "Miss Winkle is sick today. I'll
be your substitute. My name is Miss
Bliss."

"Look at her jingly bracelets," said Katie.

"And her sparkly shoes," whispered JoJo.

"Wow!" said Katie. "Miss Bliss is fancy."

"Oh, Miss Bliss," said Katie, "can I be your assistant today? I know everything."

"That's okay," said Miss Bliss. "I have lots of lesson plans."

"Let's start with math," she said. "Who can solve this problem?"

"Me!" yelled Katie.

But Miss Bliss picked Pedro. "Good work!" she praised him.

"I knew the answer, too," sighed Katie.

Miss Bliss picked Sophie to lead the line to recess.

"Miss Bliss likes Sophie because she's fancy," said Katie. "Sophie sparkles."

After recess, Katie said,
"Oh, Miss Bliss, I have a fancy
notebook. Can I show it to you?"

"Not now," said Miss Bliss. "It's
time for silent reading."

"I don't think Miss Bliss likes me,"
said Katie. "I want Miss Winkle back.
I wish it was tomorrow."

After lunch, Miss Bliss said, "It's time for music. Who wants to help pass out the instruments?"

Katie raised her hand.

"You may do it," said Miss Bliss.

"Yay!" Katie smiled. "Miss Bliss finally picked me."

But Katie was so excited, she dropped everything.

*Bam!* went the drums.

*Bling! Ring!* went the cymbals.

What a racket!

"Dopey girl," said Roddy.

Katie felt totally dopey.

The class began singing, "Row, row, row your boat."

Sophie stood close to Miss Bliss. She shook her tambourine and her pretty curls. Miss Bliss smiled at her.

"I wish Miss Bliss would smile at me," said Katie.

Next it was time for art. Katie decided, "I'll paint Binky. He always cheers me up."

But Binky was gone! Someone had opened his cage.

Everyone looked for Binky.

Katie looked the hardest.

*Whoops!* She slipped on some paint and fell down.

And that's when she found Binky!
He was sleeping in the book basket on
top of *Harold and the Purple Crayon.*
"Yay!" everyone cheered.

"Yech!" yelled Sophie. "Katie is a mess! Her shirt is stained, and she has paint on her face. Katie should go home right now!"

"Katie should stay right here," said Miss Bliss. "She is cheerful and helpful, and that is the best!"

"Really?" asked Katie. "Is that as good as fancy?"

"For sure!" said Miss Bliss. "Being your teacher is fun."

"Wow!" said Katie. "I can't wait to tell Miss Winkle!"

Miss Bliss smiled. "I think she already knows."

And she did!

# Keep Dancing, Katie

Katie loved to dance. She and JoJo
were in a class together.

Katie bragged, "I'm a fabulous
dancer!"

"I'm not a great dancer," said JoJo.
"But that's okay. I love to dance. It
makes me happy."

One day, Miss Kelly said, "Class, I have some good news. In a few weeks, we are having a show."

"Yay!" shouted Katie. "It's fun dancing on the stage!"

JoJo asked, "What music will we use?"

"'You Are My Sunshine,'" said Miss Kelly.

"I love that song," said Katie. She leaped high. She spun fast. Nobody could dance like Katie.

Then a new girl joined the class.
Her name was Mattie.

At first, Katie liked her, but not for
long.

Mattie jumped higher than Katie. She could spin faster too.

It made Katie sad. She told JoJo, "I'm not the best anymore."

"Don't be sad," said JoJo. "You are still terrific!"

Miss Kelly
played, "You are
my sunshine, my
only sunshine."

It was such
a happy song.
Mattie smiled as
she danced.

Katie did not.

"Oops!" said JoJo. "I keep falling down."

"That's okay," said Miss Kelly. "The important thing is to keep dancing. Just do the best you can."

Mattie showed JoJo how to dance without falling.

JoJo was getting better. She had a great time.

Katie did not.

Finally, it was time for the show.
"I don't feel well," Katie said.

"You look fine," said her mom. "I know you will be terrific today."

"I'm not so sure," Katie sighed.

JoJo and Mattie were very excited.

"This will be fun," said Mattie.

But then —

"Uh-oh," said Mattie, looking
worried. "I can't find my ballet shoes!"

Katie saw the shoes. They were under a backpack.

"Hmm," thought Katie. "If Mattie can't find her shoes, she can't dance. Then I'll be the best again."

Katie sat on top of the backpack.

Mattie searched for her shoes.
JoJo helped her. They searched and
searched.

"Oh, Katie," said JoJo, "have you seen Mattie's shoes?"

"Um, no," said Katie.

JoJo looked hard at Katie. Katie looked away.

Mattie began to cry. Katie tried to
look away, but she couldn't.

"I feel stinky," she said. "*Very*
stinky."

It was not a fun feeling.

Katie jumped up, saying, "Mattie! I found your shoes."

"Thank you!" said Mattie.

"I wasn't going to tell you," confessed Katie.

"But you did," said JoJo.

"And I'm glad." Katie smiled.

Katie and JoJo and Mattie hurried
to the stage. Katie leaped high. Katie
spun fast.

It was her best dancing ever.

She and JoJo and Mattie held hands as they took a bow. The audience clapped and cheered, so they took another bow.

"You were all terrific," said Miss Kelly. "I'm proud of you!"

Katie felt proud too. She sang "You Are My Sunshine" all the way home.

# Having Fun with Katie Woo!

## Boot-and-Spur Sammie

Horseback riding works up an appetite! This boot-shaped sandwich is the perfect snack after a day on a ranch. Ask a grown-up for help and don't forget to wash your hands!

### Ingredients:

- Two pieces of wheat bread
- Peanut butter
- Fruit strip

### Other things you need:

- butter knife
- kitchen scissors
- boot-shaped cookie cutter (optional)
- small star-shaped cookie cutter

## What you do:

1. With the butter knife, make a peanut-butter sandwich with the two pieces of bread.

2. Using the butter knife (rinse it off first) or a boot-shaped cookie cutter, cut out a boot from the sandwich. (You can eat the outside parts, too, so just set those to the side.)

3. Using the kitchen scissors, cut six small triangles from your fruit strip. Line them up along the outside of the boot, three on each side, to make a pattern, as in the picture.

4. Using either a star-shaped cookie cutter or the kitchen scissors, cut a star from the fruit strip. Connect the star to the boot using a bit of crust from the outside part of the sandwich.

You can add jelly in your sandwich if you prefer PB&J. Serve with a tall glass of milk for a real cowgirl treat!

# Tutu Toppers

After a wonderful dance show, it's nice to have a little party, and cupcakes make the best party food! You can make cute cupcake toppers using clean cupcake papers. Here's how:

## What you need for each topper:

- 1 cupcake liner
- 1 straw cut to 4 inches long
- card stock that matches the liners
- glue
- tape
- optional: stickers, markers, etc.

## What you do:

1. For each topper, fold the cupcake liner in half. Then cut a small half circle to make the waist opening of the tutu.

2. Using the leotard in the illustration on the opposite page as an example, cut a leotard shape from your card stock. You can ask a grown-up for help, because this is a little tricky!

3. Glue the cupcake liner to the leotard. Decorate your leotard and tutu with drawings or stickers.

4. Tape the leotard onto a straw. Now it's ready to be stuck in a freshly baked cupcake. Yum!

Download and print a sheet of ready-to-cut leotard shapes at:

www.capstonekids.com/characters/Katie-Woo

# About the Author

Fran Manushkin is the author of many popular picture books, including *Baby, Come Out!*; *Latkes and Applesauce: A Hanukkah Story*; *The Tushy Book*; *The Belly Book*; and *Big Girl Panties*. There is a real Katie Woo — she's Fran's great-niece — but she never gets in half the trouble of the Katie Woo in the books. Fran writes on her beloved Mac computer in New York City, without the help of her two naughty cats, Chaim and Goldy.

# About the Illustrator

Tammie Lyon began her love for drawing at a young age while sitting at the kitchen table with her dad. She continued her love of art and eventually attended the Columbus College of Art and Design, where she earned a bachelors degree in fine art. After a brief career as a professional ballet dancer, she decided to devote herself full time to illustration. Today she lives with her husband, Lee, in Cincinnati, Ohio. Her dogs, Gus and Dudley, keep her company as she works in her studio.